MEET BENTLEY

Written By

Lori Babb

Meet Bentley and the series to follow is lovingly dedicated in memory of our Golden Retriever Emma who lost her battle to cancer at a young age.

The first book in this series, Meet Bentley, is also dedicated to my loving husband, Kevin Babb. Thank you for always believing in my dreams and supporting my overwhelming passion for our fur babies. I am forever grateful for you.

Hi! My name is Bentley. I am a Labrador puppy. My Mommy says I am a big boy to just be a puppy.

I like to start my day with breakfast.
Sometimes I beg and slobber wanting
Moms bacon.
Do you like bacon?
What do you eat for breakfast?

After breakfast, I love to go on a long walk and sniff the flowers.
What color is your favorite flower?

I have 2 furry siblings. My big brother is a yellow Labrador named Beaudrou & a little brown Labradoodle sister named Baylee.
Is your family big or small?

My favorite hobby is chasing lizards and frogs in my yard.
What is your favorite hobby?
Do you like lizards or frogs?

After running in my backyard I like to
jump in the pool. My Dad laughs and
says I swim more than he does.
Do you like to swim? Where do you swim?
In a pool or a Lake?

Mommy loves to give me doggy cookies for being a good boy. She makes me sit and I shake my paw for my favorite treat.

What is your favorite snack?

Chasing my big red ball gives me lots of exercise. I love to jump up high and catch my ball.

What is your favorite exercise?

What is your favorite toy?

I love dinner time. After playing all day I work up an appetite. My food comes in a doggy bowl.

What is your favorite food for dinner? Do you cook it or have it delivered?

When it's bedtime I snuggle up with my bone and my teddy bear and fall fast asleep.
Good night my new friends.

Love, Bentley

"The story Meet Bentley was created in memory of our Golden Retriever Emma that lost her battle to cancer. This particular book is the beginning of a series of Bentleys adventures to help parents/adults communicate with their young children. Asking questions at the end of each page helps open up communication levels and start conversations with your little one that requires more than a yes or no answer. I hope this leads to great relationships and a few giggles as you enjoy Bentley and his silly ways."

"Bentley is a real 3 year old black Labrador Retriever that lives and plays in the Panhandle of Florida."

To Baby
Aleksander ♡

Love,
Bentley

Made in the USA
Coppell, TX
16 September 2021